THE
BIG-WIDE-
MOUTHED
TOAD-FROG
AND OTHER STORIES

Compiled by Mary Medlicott
Illustrated by Sue Williams

Kingfisher

For Tom and David M.M.
For my mother, Patricia Williams S.W.

KINGFISHER
An imprint of Larousse plc
New Penderel House, 283-288 High Holborn
London WC1V 7HZ

First published by Kingfisher 1996
2 4 6 8 10 9 7 5 3

Material in this edition was originally published
by Kingfisher in 1991 in *Time for Telling*

A CIP catalogue record for this book
is available from the British Library.

ISBN 0 7534 0002 2

Printed in Hong Kong

CONTENTS

The Big-Wide-Mouthed Toad-Frog

A North American story

•

Patrick Ryan

One fine day long ago when birds did talk and beasts did sing and grasshoppers did spit tobacco, two young ones named Jack and Mary went out for a walk.

Jack and Mary walked for the longest time. They walked further than you could tell me and further than I could tell you. They walked up over hills and mountains and down through the dark green woods. And as they walked, they talked.

"Ah now, Jack," says Mary. "Wouldn't it be good if we should catch a creature and keep it as a pet?"

"Ah now, Mary," says Jack. "It would be good. But what creature shall we catch?"

"One not very big," declared Mary.

"Nor very small," declared Jack.

"One not very tame," cried Mary.

"Yet not very wild," cried Jack.

"Well, there's only one thing to do," said Mary.

"And what is that?" asked Jack.

"Set a trip-trap," Mary said, "to catch a creature to be our pet. And I know how to do just that."

So Mary showed Jack how to set a trip-trap. Twelve sticks they gathered from the green-willow tree, long and strong and narrow as could be. Mary gathered six sticks and Jack a half-a-dozen more, and they wove together the first four. The next four sticks round the first ones were bound, and the last four tied the trigger for the trip-trap down.

Then Jack went home, and so did Mary. They left the trip-trap sit for all the night. Come the morning light the two friends ran, over hill and mountain, into the dark green wood, to see what creature the trip-trap did trap.

And lo and behold the creature it held was not very big nor yet very small, neither tame nor wild was it. It was round and wet and slimy and green, with tiny eyes and great big hind legs, and the widest big-wide mouth that ever was seen.

"Look!" said Mary.

"Look!" said Jack.

"Our trip-trap has trapped a round, wet, slimy, green BIG-WIDE-MOUTHED TOAD-FROG!'

And so it had.

And Jack and Mary they lifted the trap, and the BIG-WIDE-MOUTHED TOAD-FROG jumped and skipped and hopped right out of that.

"HELLO! (gulp) HELLO! (gulp) HELLO!" shouted the Big-Wide-Mouthed Toad-Frog. "WHAT ARE YOU AND WHAT DO YOU EAT?"

"How-do," said Mary. "I'm a little girl named Mary. And I like to eat nuts and berries and apples and cherries and hominy and corn pone and succotash and sandwiches of cheese and fish and chips and ice cream and cake."

"(Gulp) OOOOO...! (gulp) AAAAAHH! (gulp) A-MAZ-ING!" said the Big-Wide-Mouthed Toad-Frog.

"Well-now," said Jack. "I'm a little boy named Jack. And I do like to eat grits and johnny cake and cracker jack and apple-y pie and peach-y cobbler and buttermilk biscuits and sausages and rashers and chips and peas and spinach and lettuce and carrots and candy-sweets."

"(Gulp) OOOOO...! (gulp) AAAAAHH! (gulp) A-MAZ-ING!" said the Big-Wide-Mouthed Toad-Frog. "WELL, (gulp) I MUST BE OFF (gulp) AND AWAY! (gulp)"

And before Jack and Mary could catch the Big-Wide-Mouthed Toad-Frog for to keep him as a pet, he was up and away with a hop, a skip, and a jump, for the Big-Wide-Mouthed Toad-Frog he wanted to see the Big-Wide-World.

Now the very first strange creature that the Big-Wide-Mouthed Toad-Frog did meet in his travels round the Big-Wide-World was a Big-Old-Brown-Fat Monster with Branches growing out of the side of her head.

"(Gulp) HELLO! (gulp) HELLO! (gulp) HELLO!" shouted the Big-Wide-Mouthed Toad-Frog. "WHAT ARE YOU AND WHAT DO YOU EAT?"

And the Monster she Moo-ed and she Moo-ed and she Moo-ed. "I am a Cow," she said. "And I like to eat thistles the colour of bright blue, and grasses and four-leaf clovers, too."

"(Gulp) OOOOO...! (gulp) AAAAAHH! (gulp) A-MAZ-ING!" shouted the Big-Wide-Mouthed Toad-Frog.

And he hopped and skipped and jumped his way on through the Big-Wide-World.

And the very next wondrous strange creature that the Big-Wide-Mouthed Toad-Frog did meet in his travels round the Big-Wide-World was a Funny Little Thing that hung upside down and had Two Heads.

"(Gulp) HELLO! (gulp) HELLO! (gulp) HELLO!" shouted the Big-Wide-Mouthed Toad-Frog. "WHAT ARE YOU AND WHAT DO YOU EAT?"

"Ho-hum," yawned the creature. Hum-ho. I'm an opossum."

"Ho-hum," yawned the baby Opossum in his mama's pouch. "Hum-ho. Me too."

"We like to eat berries and cherries and roots and twigs," they replied.

"(Gulp) OOOOO...! (gulp) AAAAAHH! (gulp) A-MAZ-ING!" shouted the Big-Wide-Mouthed Toad-Frog.

And he hopped and skipped and jumped his way on through the Big-Wide-World.

So the next Odd Beast that he saw was as Big as a Mountain and covered with a Fur Rug.

"(Gulp) HELLO! (gulp) HELLO! (gulp) HELLO!" shouted the Big-Wide-Mouthed Toad-Frog. "WHAT ARE YOU AND WHAT DO YOU EAT?"

"Grrrr!" growled the beast. "I'm a Big Brown Bear. And I love to eat honey and fish and more fish and more honey."

"(Gulp) OOOOO...! (gulp) AAAAAHH! (gulp) A-MAZ-ING!" shouted the Big-Wide-Mouthed Toad-Frog.

And he hopped and skipped and jumped his way on through the Big-Wide-World.

Well, the next Queer Creature the Big-Wide-Mouthed Toad-Frog did meet in his journey across the Big-Wide-World was a Scary-Looking-Fellow with a Bushy-Stripy Tail and a Black Mask round his eyes – just like a robber bandit!

"(Gulp) HELLO! (gulp) HELLO! (gulp) HELLO!" shouted the Big-Wide-Mouthed Toad-Frog. "WHAT ARE YOU AND WHAT DO YOU EAT?"

And the fellow told him, "I'm a raccoon. I love to eat GARBAGE, RUBBISH and TRASH, the smellier the better!"

"(Gulp) OOOOO...! (gulp) AAAAAHH! (gulp) DIS-GUS-TING!" shouted the Big-Wide-Mouthed Toad-Frog.

And he hopped and skipped and jumped his way on through the Big-Wide-World.

Now the last monstrous beast the Big-Wide-Mouthed Toad-Frog did spy on his travels was a Long Green Log with a Great Big Smile who rolled and slithered along on his belly.

"(Gulp) HELLO! (gulp) HELLO! (gulp) HELLO!" shouted the Big-Wide-Mouthed Toad-Frog. "WHAT ARE YOU AND WHAT DO YOU EAT?"

And the Smiling Log smiled a Great-Big-Wide-Mouthed Smile and he said, "Heh heh heh. I'm an alligator! And I just LOVE to eat BIG-WIDE-MOUTHED TOAD-FROGS!" said the alligator. "Have YOU seen any BIG-WIDE-MOUTHED TOAD-FROGS about?"

And the Big-Wide-Mouthed Toad-Frog's eyes got VERY VERY BIG and his Big-Wide-Mouth closed up and got very very small and the Big-Wide-Mouthed Toad-Frog said with a squeak, "Nope, I've not seen any such thing as a Big-Wide-Mouthed Toad-Frog ever, not at all round here, not ever in all my life!'

Then the Big-Wide-Mouthed Toad-Frog hopped and skipped and jumped his way all the way back to Jack and Mary's trip-trap, as fast as he could hop and skip and jump. And in that trip-trap he stayed most merrily, and lived there a most long time for his life, because the Big-Wide-Mouthed Toad-Frog had learned an ever so important lesson: that it sometimes pays to keep a BIG WIDE MOUTH SHUT!

The Very Mean King

A Kenyan story
•
Sandra A. Agard

There was once a Very Mean King
who sat on his throne all day long
and laughed in a wicked way.
HEE, HEE, HEE.
When he was not laughing,
he was rubbing his hands together.
RUB, RUB, RUB.
When he was not rubbing his hands
together, he was stamping his feet.
STAMP, STAMP, STAMP.
And when he was not stamping his feet, he was growling.
GROWL, GROWL, GROWL.

He never smiled.

He never laughed.

He never danced.

And because he never smiled, laughed or danced, he never allowed his people to smile, laugh or dance.

In fact, he had some very mean-looking guards who snarled and hissed all day. SNARL, SNARL, HISS, HISS. And if the Very Mean King caught anyone smiling, laughing or dancing he would order his very mean-looking guards to whip the people.

WHIP, WHIP, WHIP.

11

So the people were sad all the time and were made to work in the Very Mean King's fields all day long under the burning hot sun.

Sometimes the Very Mean King would not let the people stop to rest or give them anything to eat. And when the people begged for food – what do you think? The Very Mean King said "NO!" in a very loud voice.

What a Very Mean King!

One day the Very Mean King slept after an enormous lunch.
SNORE, SNORE, SNORE.

And the guards guarded, looking as mean as ever.

Up in the sky there lived the Sparrow who had been watching the earth for a long time and had seen how meanly the Very Mean King was treating his people. So she decided it was time the Very Mean King was taught a lesson.

So from its very special secret place amongst the clouds she took the Rattle of Punishment and flew down to earth.

She cast a very special secret spell that made her invisible and as she flew the Rattle began to play beautiful music. When the people heard the music they instantly stopped what they were doing and found that their lips began to twitch, their feet were tingling and their hips began to wriggle and before they could stop themselves they were smiling, laughing and dancing.

They could not stop.

They smiled and smiled.

They laughed and laughed.

They danced and danced all over the Very Mean King's fields.

Well, the smiling, laughing and dancing woke up the Very Mean King and when he looked out of the window and saw what the people were doing he sent his mean-looking guards out to stop them.

But no sooner had the guards arrived at the fields, they too began to smile, laugh and dance.

So the Very Mean King went himself and in a loud voice shouted, "STOP!"

He shouted so loud it shook the very foundations of the earth.

The Sparrow stopped playing and everybody stopped smiling, laughing and dancing. They ran away and hid.

The Very Mean King looked at his fields. They were all trampled and completely ruined.

This time he roared a huge roar, "ROARRRRRR!"

And he was just about to call out his army to capture the people when the Sparrow appeared before him and said, "You have been a very mean king and for that you will be punished."

And she shook the Rattle of Punishment and this time only the Very Mean King smiled, laughed or danced.

He smiled, laughed and danced for THREE DAYS and THREE NIGHTS until he begged the Sparrow to stop.

He fell on the ground exhausted.

The people came out of their hiding places and waited.

The Very Mean King got up and looked at his people. He remembered how happy they had seemed when they smiled, laughed and danced and he bowed his head in shame. Then, in a very kingly voice, he said, "My people, I've been a very mean king. From now on I'm going to be a good king."

So he gave his people food and they smiled, laughed and danced. So did the guards, for they were getting a little tired of snarling and hissing all day and had rather enjoyed singing, laughing and dancing in the fields.

The Sparrow flew away taking with her the magic Rattle of Punishment, placing it back in its special secret place.

But who knows when she might come back again and who will dance that special magic dance?

COULD IT BE YOU?

Loawnu Mends the Sky

A Chinese story

●

Vivienne Corringham

A long time ago, the world was new. It had just been made, and do you know, they still hadn't got some things in the world exactly right. And one of the things they hadn't got right was the sky. Let me tell you what happened.

One sunny day in China, some children went out to play. They were running around in their favourite field when suddenly – PLOP! – a flat blue thing with raggedy edges fell just near them. Over there – PLOP! – and here – PLOP! – and then – PLOP! PLOP! PLOP! Things were falling all over their field and in the fields around. What do you think they were? The children looked up. Oh, how terrible! Pieces of sky were falling down, and leaving behind great big holes. You could see right inside the sky. Out of the holes oozed thick black clouds spreading like ink in water, and turning the sky from blue to black.

"What shall we do?" they asked each other.

Well, in those days, if you had a problem you went to see the local wise woman, and in this village her name was Loawnu. So they ran up the hill to her house and they rushed through the door, shouting, "Loawnu, what are we going to do? The sky's falling down!"

"Well now," said Loawnu, "why don't you try to find all the pieces of sky that have fallen and then I can mend it."

What a good idea! Off they went and picked up all the bits that were lying on the ground but they couldn't see any more. Can you think of any places where those pieces might be hiding? Yes, they found some down a well, one stuck in a bamboo tree, and another on the roof of a house.

So these friends gathered all the bits they could find – there were lots of them – and carried them up the hill to Loawnu, and she began to count them. It took a long time. Then she went outside and counted the holes in the sky where the bits had fallen out. At the end she said, "I'm afraid there are still some bits missing. Maybe they sank to the bottom of the sea where we'll never find them. I'll put all the pieces you found back into the sky, but we'll need something else to fill in the gaps."

"Why?" asked the children. "Will the gaps matter?"

"Have you ever had a jigsaw puzzle," began Loawnu,

"with a piece missing? You know how it never works without that piece. It's the same with the sky. We'll have to fill in the holes somehow. Ah, but listen! I've had a wonderful idea. Just look at all these coloured stones on the ground."

The children looked around at them.

"That's what I'll use. I can put some red ones in this part of the sky and then, look, I'll use a ring of those purple ones, and maybe I can have some green dots and an orange stripe over there. Won't the sky look pretty!"

But the children's faces had fallen. They wanted a blue sky. "We don't like all those bright colours. The sky's always been blue all day and black all night," they wailed.

Loawnu looked thoughtful for a minute and then she said, "All right. I promise you this. When you wake up tomorrow morning, the sky will be as blue as it always was. Now leave it to me."

So the children went home, and Loawnu built a tall ladder and mended the sky.

The next morning, as soon as the children awoke, they ran out and looked up at the sky. There it was, blue as blue. They couldn't see any holes. They couldn't see any gaps. One little boy went up to Loawnu.

"You're so clever," he said. "I think you used blue cloth and stitched it over the holes. Did you? Did you?"

Loawnu smiled but she said nothing. How do you think she'd done it? Well, she wouldn't tell them and they didn't really mind, because the sky was blue again.

But do you know what happened that night? The smallest girl in the village couldn't sleep because it was too hot. So she went outside for some air, and when she opened the door she couldn't believe her eyes. She could see what Loawnu had used to fill up the holes in the sky, and if you go out at night you'll see too.

Now, I told you the world was still new, and until then the sky had always been plain blue in the day and plain black at night. But it wasn't plain black that night, oh no. The little girl shouted as loudly as she could and the whole village came running. Their mouths fell open with amazement. What do you think they saw?

STARS!

There they were, silver and shining. Loawnu had put one in each of the holes in the sky.

"Aha! That's why she told us to come in the *morning* and the sky would look the same as ever," said one little boy. "It's true, you can't see stars in the daytime, can you, and she didn't say the sky would look the same at night!"

Nobody had ever seen stars before, and so they stood and watched them twinkling and glittering. Some people stayed there all night, and the more they watched, the more they liked them. Everybody agreed the night seemed friendlier now that there were stars.

So that is how Loawnu mended the sky.

The Hedgehog's Race

A Scottish travellers' tale

•

Duncan Williamson

If you were to travel the hills of Scotland today you would find that hedgehogs and hares live together. They're great friends. It wasn't always so...

Every morning early, old Mr Brown Hare came down from his bed in the hillside. He was bound for the farmer's field because his breakfast was turnips. He loved the young turnips coming up, the leaves. But this one morning, bright and early, as old Mr Hare came popping down the hillside, a beautiful sunny morning, the first person he met was old Mr Hedgehog. And he was crawling around the hedgerows hunting for *his* breakfast! Snails and slugs and worms which hedgehogs love to eat. Because Mr Hare was feeling very frisky this morning, he rubbed his paws together and said to himself, "Oh ho, old Mr Hedgehog! I'm going to have some fun to myself this morning!" He liked to tease old Mr Hedgehog, you know!

So when he came down to the gate leading to the farmer's field old Mr Hedgehog of course sat up with his wee pointed nose and his little short legs. And old Mr Hare said, "Good morning, Short Legs!"

And like that off went Mr Hare for his breakfast in the farmer's turnip field.

But what do you think old Mr Hedgehog did? He toddled away back to his little nest where his old wife lived, old Mrs Hedgehog! And he said, "My dear, would you do something for me?"

Of course, old Mrs Hedgehog she loved her old husband Mr Hedgehog very much. She said, "Of course, husband, I'll do anything for you!"

He said, "You see, my dear, I've challenged Mr Hare to a race."

She said, "Husband, have you gone out of your mind? Have you gone crazy?"

"No, my dear, I've not gone crazy. But," he said, "if you will agree to help me, with your help I will teach old Mr Hare a lesson he will never forget."

She said, "What do you want me to do, husband?"

"Well," he said, "it's so simple! You know, old Mr Hare thinks he's very clever. But he's not as clever as he thinks he is. Because, like everyone else, he doesn't know you from me." (Neither do I! If you met two hedgehogs, you wouldn't know a Mr from a Mrs, would you?)

"Well," she said, "husband, what do you want me to do?"

He said, "My dear, all I want you to do is... I want you to wait till daybreak. I will wait up at the top of the gate till Mr Hare comes down from the hillside, from his bush. And I will challenge him to a race. But I'm not going to run any, and neither are you! I want you to wait at the foot of the field. And when old Mr Hare comes down to the foot of the field all you have to do is just stand up and say, "I'm here before you!" And I will wait up at the top of the gate and I won't move. Silly old Mr Hare will never know you from me!" So the plan was made.

That night, after giving her old husband Mr Hedgehog a little cuddle, off she went. And she wandered away down to the foot of the field. There she waited. It was summer time, the nights were not very long. And of course old Mr Hare was very bright in the morning. He liked to be up early, half past four when the sun came up! So old Mr Hedgehog he crawled away to the gate and there he waited. He never looked for a worm, he never looked for a snail. He waited for Mr Hare!

But soon as the sun began to rise, down came old Mr Hare so proud of himself. He was going to show old Mr Hedgehog this morning how to run! Like he'd never run before in all his life. And then he was going to go on calling him Short Legs every time they met. See? And many other things forbyes. Slow Coach and things like that! So when Mr Hare came to the gate, there sat old Mr Hedgehog.

He said, "Good morning, Short Legs, are you ready?"

Of course, Mr Hedgehog, who was very sensitive about his short legs, said, "You promised you wouldn't call me Short Legs any more!"

He said, "Of course, I promised you – but after the race! You've not beat me yet. And you don't have one single chance in this world. I'm going to beat you, and this morning because I feel so frisky I'm going to show you what it's like to run! After I beat you I'm going to go on calling you Short Legs all your life and many other things forbyes!"

"Well," said old Mr Hedgehog, thinking to himself, "she'll be at the bottom of the field by this time." He was happy. He said, "OK, Mr Hare, are you ready?"

And Mr Hare said, "As ready as I'll ever be!" He rubbed his paws together and said, "One, two, three – off we go!"

And old Mr Hare, off he flew down that field faster than he'd ever run. Old Mr Hedgehog sat there and watched him running like he'd never run before in his life. But he was in for a big surprise. When he came to the foot of the field there in front of him was old Mrs Hedgehog.

She said, "I'm here before you!"

And quick as a light old Mr Hare he turned and he ran back up the field as fast as he could. But on the way up he ran faster! When he came to the top of the field, there was old Mr Hedgehog.

And old Mr Hedgehog said, "I'm here before you!"

Quick as a light old Mr Hare he turned again and down that field he ran, faster than he ever ran before! But when he came to the foot of the field there was old Mrs Hedgehog!

She said, "I'm here before you!" And of course poor old Mr Hare, not knowing Mrs Hedgehog from Mr Hedgehog, he turned again! Up that field he flew as fast as he could run.

But then old Mr Hedgehog said, "I'm still here before you!"

So up and down and up and down ran old Mr Hare. Till at last he was completely exhausted. He could not run another step. He came up to the top of the field and he was lying there, his tongue hanging out. And he was panting.

He said, "Tell me, Mr Hedgehog, tell me, please! How in the world did you ever do it? You ran so fast I never even saw you pass me by!"

"Of course," said old Mr Hedgehog, "I told you! You wouldn't believe me that you don't need long legs to run fast, you know!"

"Well," said old Mr Hare, "you really beat me there and I'm still not sure how you did it, but I promise you, my friend, I will never call you Short Legs again as long as I live!"

And that's why today, if you're up in the gorse hills, in the woods, you will find hedgehogs and hares asleep in the same bush – because they are very good friends! And as for old Mr Hare, he never called Mr Hedgehog Short Legs again. But of course you and I know that he beat him by a trick, didn't he? But we ain't going to tell Mr Hare, are we?

Rainbow Bird

An Aboriginal story

●

Eric Maddern

A long time ago, so the old people say, there was a big, big, big, Crocodile. He had tough, scaly skin and razorsharp teeth, and he was really, really mean. And this Crocodile Man had one thing no one else had. Just like a dragon he had fire! But he used to sit by his billabong all day long and keep the fire to himself. "I'm boss for fire," he would growl at the other animals. "I'm boss for fire."

Now in a nearby tree lived the Plain Bird Woman. Plain Bird Woman had no light. At night she slept beside no camp fire and she had to eat her food – her fish, her lizards and her mussels – all raw! Ugh! She didn't like the taste very much, but every time she asked Crocodile Man if she could have some fire she was knocked away.

"But what about people?" she said. "Are they to eat their food raw?"

"They can eat it raw," said the gruff old Crocodile Man. "I will not give you my firesticks. I'm boss for fire."

Plain Bird Woman flew up to the nearby tree and watched Crocodile Man. She wished and wished she could have fire to cook her food and keep herself warm. Then she thought, Maybe I could just fly down and sn...sn...sn...snatch the fire from the cr...cr...cr...crocodile." She was very frightened but she got herself ready and then flew down.

"Oh no, no, no, NO!" roared the Crocodile Man. "You're just a little bird. Me, I'm a big crocodile. You must eat your food raw!"

"You're so mean," sighed Plain Bird Woman. "If I had fire I'd give it to you." And she flew back into the tree.

Time passed. Plain Bird Woman watched and waited, waited and watched. Then one day she saw Crocodile Man open his jaws and give a big yawn. "Now's my chance," she thought, and she flashed down from the tree, snatched the firesticks and flew up into the air. And there was nothing the Crocodile Man could do about it.

"Now I have light, now I can cook fish and now I shall give fire to people," said Plain Bird Woman happily. And she flew around the country putting fire at the heart of every tree, one by one. Then she flew back to Crocodile Man and said, "Now you must stay down there in the wet places. I'll fly high in the dry places. I'll be a bird. I'll stay on top. If you come up here you might die!"

And then Plain Bird Woman put the firesticks into her tail, and that's where they are today. She looked so beautiful, with the colours of fire in her feathers, that everyone called her 'Rainbow Bird'. Even today, in Australia, she's known as the 'Rainbow Lorikeet'.

And now if you want to make fire, what do you need?

Matches! And what are the matches made from? Wood! And where does the wood come from? Trees! And what's in the heart of the tree? Fire! And who put the fire into the heart of the tree? The Rainbow Bird!

Papa Bwa Greedy Guest

A story from Dominica

•

Jane Grell

A woodcutter came home one night with a very strange old man. His hair was thick and tangled like a wild overgrown garden. His bushy grey beard was so long it almost touched the ground.

"This is Papa Bwa," said the woodcutter, introducing the old man to his wife, Nana. "His job is to protect the forest and everything in it. At least that's what he told me."

"Then why have you brought him here?" asked his wife, not very pleased to see the old man.

"He is very, very hungry," replied the wood-cutter, "so I've invited him to supper."

Nana his wife could not easily turn away a hungry old man from her house, but she was far from happy.

"Hmm!" she said at last. "He'll have to wash and change into something cleaner. There's a tub of water out there," she said to the old man and pointed to the yard. "And you better put these on." She handed him an old pair of clean overalls.

After he had washed and changed she was still not satisfied. She looked the old man up and down and sucked her teeth in disgust.

"Chut, man, this beard has got to go. There must be a million bugs and fleas hiding in there. I'm not having them crawling all over my house, you hear."

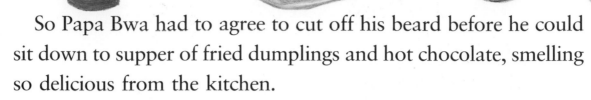

So Papa Bwa had to agree to cut off his beard before he could sit down to supper of fried dumplings and hot chocolate, smelling so delicious from the kitchen.

After supper Papa Bwa curled up on a small sofa and went to sleep.

At breakfast the next morning a very odd thing happened. When Nana gave Papa Bwa a mug of tea, he drank the tea and ate the mug.

At lunchtime Nana gave him fried plantains and flying fish on a dish. Papa Bwa ate the food and devoured the dish.

At suppertime Nana gave him calaloo and crab in a calabash. Papa Bwa gobbled up the calaloo and crab and polished off the calabash.

The next morning Nana gave him tea in a zinc jug. He gulped down the tea and crunched away the jug.

At lunch that day Nana gave him rice and peas and avocado on a plate. He wolfed down the rice and peas and avocado and munched away the plate.

That night Nana gave him supper of pigeon peas with curried salt fish in a wooden washing-up bowl. Papa Bwa enjoyed the pigeon peas and curried salt fish then guzzled up the washing-up bowl.

Papa Bwa stayed several days with the woodcutter and his wife and during that time he ate his way through several mugs, jugs, a calabash, a washing-up bowl, a bucket and even a pig's trough.

Nana was very upset. One night she said to her husband, "Tomorrow, you must take this . . . creature back to the woods where you found him and leave him there."

"But supposing he follows me back?" said the woodcutter.

"You found him," yelled his wife impatiently, "you get rid of him. If you don't, we won't have a single cup or plate left in this house. The way he's going, who knows? He'll eat all the furniture, then the house and he will surely eat us as well."

For once the woodcutter listened to his wife. He did not want his chairs, table and bed to be eaten. He did not much want his wife to be eaten and he certainly did not like the idea of being eaten himself.

So early in the morning he told Papa Bwa that it was time to return to his home in the forest as he made his wife very unhappy.

Papa Bwa went quietly with the woodcutter until they reached the spot in the woods where they had met, then he demanded to have his beard back. "I will not go without my beard!" he shrieked.

"But that's impossible," replied the woodcutter. "Your beard has been cut off and is lying on a rubbish heap under a mango tree."

But the old man only stamped his feet shouting, "I don't care!"
Then he started jumping up and down, up and down in front of the
woodcutter, chanting:

"CRICK! CRACK!
BREAK MY BACK
I WANT MY BEARD
AND THAT IS THAT."

Suddenly, from somewhere in the forest, appeared three
wise old women of the woods. They wanted to know what the
argument was about, so the woodcutter told them everything
and Papa Bwa finished up with:

"CRICK! CRACK!
BREAK MY BACK
I WANT MY BEARD
AND THAT IS THAT."

The three wise women of the woods shrieked with laughter and
delight and they too started to jump around singing:

"CRICK! CRACK!
BREAK HIS BACK
HE WANTS HIS BEARD
AND THAT IS THAT."

Well, they chanted and clapped and danced round and
round the poor woodcutter until he was quite dizzy.

Just then a bird swept down from the tree tops. It was Siflet Montagne, the beautiful whistling bird of the mountains. She was curious to know what all the singing and dancing was about. So the woodcutter told the whole story all over again, finished off by Papa Bwa with:

> "CRICK! CRACK!
> BREAK MY BACK
> I WANT MY BEARD
> AND THAT IS THAT."

helped along by the three wise women of the woods with:

> "CRICK! CRACK!
> BREAK HIS BACK
> HE WANTS HIS BEARD
> AND THAT IS THAT."

The mountain whistler felt sorry for the woodcutter and wanted to help him. So she whistled in her most melodious voice while the dancers whirled and swirled, danced and pranced, jigged and jogged to the fabulous tune of this enchanting bird.

Then the mountain whistler hovered close to the woodcutter and whispered, "I will whistle for a little while more. When they are not looking, you must seize your chance and run for it, man."

Then the bird sang more sweetly and the dancers danced more quickly as they followed her down the path.

"CRICK! CRACK!
BREAK MY BACK
I WANT MY BEARD
AND THAT IS THAT."

And as they skipped and bopped, hipped and hopped, wheeled and turned, led away by the whistling bird, the woodcutter saw his chance and VOOP! he slipped away towards his own cottage. But he hadn't gone very far when Papa Bwa and the three wise women of the woods realized what was happening. VOOP! they left the mountain whistler and began to chase the woodcutter, who ran and ran and ran, and never stopped until he was safely home. There, his wife Nana was standing in the open doorway. He rushed in, pulling her along with him and bolted the door just in the nick of time, the nick of time, leaving his shirt in the grasping hands of the fastest wise woman of the woods.

From that day on, the woodcutter and his wife have been *very* careful about inviting strangers home to supper.

Mashenka and the Bear

A Russian story

•

James Riordan

An old peasant and his wife had a granddaughter, Mashenka. One summer's day, the little girl's friends called on her to go mushrooming with them in the meadow.

"Grannie, Grandad," cried Mashenka. "May I go out to play? I'll bring you lots of mushrooms, I promise."

"Run along then," the old pair said, "but mind you don't go near the forest or else the wolves or bears will get you."

Off skipped the girls towards the meadow at the forest edge. Mashenka knew that the best and biggest mushrooms grew beneath the trees and bushes in the forest. Almost without noticing it, she wandered out of sight of her friends. She moved from tree to tree, from bush to bush, picking a basketful of mushrooms – reds and yellows, browns and whites. All the while she went deeper and deeper into the forest. Suddenly, she looked up and realized she was lost.

"Hell-oooo! Hell-oooo!" she called.

There was no reply.

Someone heard her nonetheless.

From the trees came a rustling and a cracking, and out stepped a big brown bear. When he set eyes on the little girl, he threw up his arms in joy.

"Aha!" he cried. "You'll make a fine servant for me, my pretty one."

Taking the girl roughly by the arm, he dragged her to his cottage in the depths of the dark wood. Once inside, he growled at her, "Now stoke the fire, cook some porridge and make my home clean and tidy."

There now began a miserable life in the bear's cottage for poor Mashenka. Day after day she toiled from dawn to dusk, afraid the bear would eat her. All the while she thought of how she could escape. Finally, an idea came to her.

"Mister Bear," she said politely, "may I go home for a day to show my grandparents I am alive and well?"

"Certainly not," growled the bear. "You'll never leave here. If you have a message I'll take it myself."

That was just what Mashenka had planned. She baked some cherry pies, piled them on a dish and fetched a big basket. Then she called the bear.

"Mister Bear, I'll put the pies in this basket for you to carry home. Remember, though, not to open the basket and don't touch the pies. I'll be watching. When you set off I'll climb on to the roof to keep an eye on you."

"All right, pretty one," grumbled the bear. "Just let me take a nap before I go."

No sooner was the bear asleep than Mashenka quickly climbed on to the roof and made a lifelike figure out of a pole, her coat and headscarf. Then she scrambled down, squeezed into the basket and pulled the dish of cherry pies over her head. When the bear woke up and saw the basket ready, he hoisted it on to his broad back and set off for the village.

Through the trees he ambled with his load and soon he felt tired and footsore. Stopping by a tree stump, he sank down to rest, thinking of eating a cherry pie. But just as he was about to open the basket, he heard Mashenka's voice.

"Don't sit there all day and don't you touch those pies."

Glancing round he could just see her figure on his roof.

"My, my, that maid has sharp eyes," he mumbled to himself.

Up he got and continued on his way.

On and on he went, carrying the heavy load. Soon he came upon another tree stump.

"I'll just take a rest and eat a cherry pie," he thought, puffing and panting. Yet once again Mashenka's muffled voice was heard.

"Don't sit down and don't touch those pies. Go straight to the village as I told you."

He looked back but could no longer see his house.

"Well, I'll be jiggered!" he exclaimed. "She's got eyes like a hawk, that girl."

So on he went.

Through the trees he shuffled, down into the valley, on through groves of ash, up grassy knolls until, finally, he emerged into a meadow.

"I must rest my poor feet," he sighed. "And I'll just have one small pie to refresh me. She surely cannot see me now."

But from out of nowhere came a distant voice.

"I can see you! I can see you! Don't you touch those cherry pies! Go on, Mister Bear."

The bear was puzzled, even scared.

"What an extraordinary girl she is," he growled, hurrying across the field.

At last he arrived at the village, stopped at Mashenka's door and knocked loudly.

"Open up, open up!" he cried gruffly. "I've brought a present from your granddaughter."

The moment they heard his voice, however, dogs came running from all the yards. Their barking startled him so much, he left the basket at the door and made off towards the forest without a backward glance.

How surprised Mashenka's grandparents were when they opened the door, found the basket and saw no one in sight.

Grandad lifted up the lid, stared hard and could scarcely believe his eyes. For there beneath the cherry pies sat the little girl, alive and well.

Grannie and Grandad both danced with joy, hugged Mashenka and said what a clever girl she was to trick the bear. Soon all her friends heard the news and came running to hug and kiss her too. Mashenka was so happy.

In the meantime, deep in the forest, the old bear had reached home and shouted to the figure on the roof to make his tea. Of course, it did not take him long to learn that the wise young girl had tricked him.

More Kingfisher Gift Collections to Enjoy

BREAKING THE SPELL:
TALES OF ENCHANTMENT
Selected by Sally Grindley
Illustrated by Susan Field

REALMS OF GOLD:
MYTHS AND LEGENDS
FROM AROUND THE WORLD
Ann Pilling
Illustrated by Kady MacDonald Denton

SOMETHING RICH AND STRANGE:
A TREASURY OF SHAKESPEARE'S VERSE
Selected by Gina Pollinger
Illustrated by Emma Chichester Clark

TALES FROM THE BALLET
Antonia Barber
Illustrated by Diz Wallis

THE KING WITH DIRTY FEET
AND OTHER STORIES
Compiled by Mary Medlicott
Illustrated by Sue Williams